THE BLOB ON THE ROCK

MICHAEL KINGSWOOD

ISBN 13: 978-1-950683-06-2

ISBN 10: 1-950683-06-0

ABOUT THIS BOOK

A scientific expedition to deep space makes a discovery that will re-shape what we believe about life in the universe.

As long as it doesn't kill them first.

The Blob On The Rock is a 5,000 word short story.

Enjoy the book! After you're done, please come to Michael's website and sign up for his mailing list at http://www.michaelkingswood.com/newsletter-signup/. Guaranteed to be spam free, he uses it to announce new releases and special promotions for his fans.

THE BLOB ON THE ROCK

"What am I looking at here?"

Margaret sounded annoyed, tired, confused, and determined all at once. She looked like hell, though Ray was not stupid enough to say so.

Instead, he activated the camera's zoom function. On the display in front of them, the image enlarged enough that there was no doubt.

"Son of a bitch," Margaret breathed, earning a nod of agreement from Ray.

"Never thought you'd see one of those, did you?" he replied, not bothering to suppress the satisfaction he felt.

Margaret had only grudgingly authorized this expedition, under the condition that she would supervise it personally. Ray had been halfway inclined to scrap the whole thing rather than endure that, but his partners forced his hand and he had reluctantly accepted the terms.

He could count on one hand the number of days, in the six months since, that he had not regretted that decision.

Margaret had made his life a living hell. Reports,

projections, assessments, re-assessments of the assessments when results did not track with expectation, formal inquiries for every little thing that went wrong, the kind of inquiries that take a man-week or more to complete and leave you with nothing more than you started with at the beginning except piles of paperwork and several days of your life gone that you would never get back—all these and more she forced on him in the name of good management, procedural compliance, or whatever buzz phrase of the day she felt like latching on to.

It had gotten to the point that in a given day, he probably got two hours of real work done, max.

But today it was all worth it, because he was right.

Hot damn, he was right!

Even Margaret would not be able to deny it. Though she would try. Of that he had no doubt.

The door to the control room opened behind them and Ray turned to see Jusef, one of his partners, stroll in. Like everyone on the ship, he wore a loose light-grey jumpsuit that was belted at the waist and soft-soled shoes. This morning, he also wore a broad grin on his face.

Nodding in greeting, Jusef quipped, "What do you think of that, Maggie? Something, isn't it?"

Margaret scowled as she looked away from the display toward Jusef. She hated being called Maggie, something she had made abundantly clear over the years. But Jusef seemed to enjoy pushing her buttons. With no escape from each other in the ship's confines, Ray had thought Jusef would ease up.

No such luck.

"Yes, very interesting," Margaret replied in a clipped tone that generally meant she was about ready to chew some ass. "But hardly conclusive, in and of itself."

Ray felt his jaw drop. "What do you mean?" he said. "What else could..."

"I can think of half a dozen explanations off the top of my head, none of which conform to your hypothesis," she replied.

Jusef snorted and opened his mouth to retort, but stopped as Ray raised a calming hand.

"What would you suggest then?" Ray asked in as polite a tone as possible.

Margaret was silent for a moment as she looked back at the display and the image that grew slowly larger as their ship approached the object. Ray could not figure how there could be any doubt, but he was forced to admit it was more prudent to proceed from a skeptical point of view, however much he might not like it.

Finally, she spoke again.

"Continue gathering data and when we get close enough, collect a sample. If this," she gestured toward the slowly rotating object in the display, "is what you think it is, we should be able to tell easily enough once we get a close look at it."

Ray blinked in surprise. He glanced at Jusef, who wore a startled expression as well, one that faded into wariness quickly.

"Is that wise?" Jusef asked, his voice for once completely serious. "We don't know where it's from or what it can do. If we expose ourselves or contaminate the ship..."

Now it was time for Margaret to snort. "We have a clean room and bio-containment. Surely your team is competent to transport it without violating any of the protocols."

That went without saying. They were all exobiologists with extensive experience studying new organisms. Even Margaret, though by virtue or her position at the National Science Foundation she spent more time pushing paper and dealing with bureaucracy than anything else lately.

But this...

"This is different than anything we've ever encountered, Margaret," Ray said. "An organism that is born, lives, and dies, assuming it is does die, all in the vacuum of space. We can't know how it will react to a strong gravity well, let alone an atmosphere, severe heat..."

"Twenty-two degrees is hardly severe."

"It is when you live in negative two hundred sixty," Jusef pointed out.

Margaret flushed with what could only be embarrassment. That was a rookie mistake for a lay person, let alone a scientist. She had been out of the game for a while, Ray thought, but still.

"I don't think bringing it onboard is a good idea," Ray said, completing his earlier thought.

Margaret sniffed. Looking back at the display, she frowned slightly, then nodded. "Very well. Let's learn everything we can from afar. We may not need a sample at all." She looked back at Ray and whatever embarrassment she had felt a moment ago was gone, replaced by a steely expression of authority. "But I want the containment prepped and ready, just in case."

With that, she stalked out of the control room. As the door slid shut behind her, Jusef chuckled. "I thought this was your project, Ray."

"So did I," Ray replied with a rueful smile.

It was his idea. He was the one who ran the

gauntlet of peer ridicule, funding pressure, and skepticism to get the expedition approved, however tight their budget ended up being.

Unfortunately, she who provides the money tends to make the rules in the real world.

"Well you heard her. Tell Charlie to get the containment facility ready."

Jusef nodded and took a step toward the door. It slid open and he paused, looking over his shoulder toward Ray. "Did you notice something?"

Ray shook his head. "No, what?"

"She gave over trying to deny what that thing is." Jusef grinned and waggled his eyebrows, then he stepped out of the room.

The door slid shut and Ray's smiled became broader, more genuinely happy. Jusef was right. How about that?

~

RAY WATCHED with growing excitement as Eva, the ship's pilot and the only non-scientist aboard, keyed in the commands to bring the ship into a parallel orbit with the object they'd been approaching.

They were close now, only a kilometer away from it, and Ray could make out every detail with only minor use of the camera's zoom feature.

The asteroid was oblong, just over a hundred meters in length and a third of that wide, and tumbled end over end in a slow, awkward-looking rotation. It was nondescript, easily overlooked as just another hunk of mostly worthless elements floating through space.

Except for the darker lumps that speckled its surface.

Even they were nothing special to look at if one did so quickly. Only observing them for a moment or two revealed that they were moving across the asteroid's surface. And as each moved, it left behind a deep rift in the rock's surface.

The creatures, whatever they were, were eating the asteroid. Ray was sure of it.

"Alright Ray, we're parked," Eva said as she tapped shut one last dialogue window on her pilot's control station. Then she turned around and gave him a warm grin. "Have fun."

"You know it," he replied, and winked back.

She chuckled and shook her head in amusement, then leaned back in her chair to watch the fireworks, such as they were.

"Jusef," Ray began.

"Already on it. Spectrographic analyzer is online." At his workstation, Jusef leaned forward, peering intently at the readout from the analyzer. "Damn. The creatures' albedo is too low to get a good reading with this ambient light level. There's not enough light to work with. I'll have to flash them." He frowned and chewed on his lip for a moment, then looked over at Ray.

Ray thought about it for a minute.

The creatures might be sensitive to light; living in space the way they did, it was only logical they would get at least some of their energy from nearby stars. He did not want to disturb or harm them. On the other hand, the analyzer's flash was brief and in a discreet frequency band, so the chance of causing undue stress was rather low.

And they needed information.

He nodded. "Ok, go ahead."

Jusef returned the nod and said, "Here goes

nothing."

He tapped a command into his workstation. A moment later, powerful lights mounted beneath the ship's hull illuminated a targeted area of the asteroid briefly. Jusef's display lit up as data streamed across it.

His eyes widened.

"Arsenic-based from the looks of it. A few complex compounds...this one looks almost like chlorophyl, but not quite." He leaned back and looked over at Ray. "It'll take a while to fully analyze, but this thing is a beauty!"

"Outstanding," Ray said, grinning. He loved being right. He really did. Glancing over at Margaret, sitting at her observation workstation in the corner, he was gratified to see her eyes wide in amazement. "Charlie?"

Off to his left, Charlie cleared his throat and replied, "Looks like they average a meter and a half long by three quarters of a meter wide. Radar mapping has them moving at an average of ten centimeters per minute and leaving a trail an average of six centimeters deep in their path. Infrared puts them at 5 degrees above background."

"Warm blooded?" Margaret said a bit breathlessly. "How is that possible in this environment?"

"That's what we're here to find out, Margaret," Ray said, hardly able to contain his excitement. He couldn't help himself. He looked back at her, winked, and quipped, "Oh ye of little faith."

She glowered at him for a moment, then smirked and nodded. "True enough. Though I don't see how you'll be able to figure that out without examining a specimen up close."

Ray sighed. "You're probably right." Looking

back at the display, he tapped his fingers on the top of his workstation desk.

Charlie piped up, "If we grab one, we'll need to take a piece of the asteroid as well. It'll be easier to just scoop it out than to try to remove the thing from the rock. I can set up the containment to simulate the exterior conditions as closely as possible. Then all we have to do is configure the sample container to maintain micro-gravity during transport in and out of containment." He smiled slightly. "Not too hard."

Ray thought about it for a minute. Despite his and Jusef's earlier resistance to Margaret's notion, he had, in the back of his mind, considered the possibility of doing an EVA to retrieve a sample of whatever they found. It was not anything he hadn't done before, really.

Still...

"What do you think, Jusef?"

Jusef frowned and leaned forward, peering at the main display through narrowed eyes. "I don't know. There's a lot that can go wrong."

"Oh please." Margaret sounded annoyed again. As usual. "Can you really tell me you'll be able to learn much more of use from way out here?" There was a brief period of silence, then she nodded to herself. "I didn't think so."

Ray and Jusef traded glances. Jusef rolled his eyes, no doubt thinking the same thing Ray was.

If only she would leave them alone to do their work, things would be so much easier.

Ray sighed. "Alright, Margaret. We'll do it your way. Charlie, prep for an EVA."

⁓

THE CREATURE RESTING on the hunk of rock in the middle of the containment area did not look like anything special. Just a green-brown blob atop a grey-brown surface.

It was the coolest thing Ray had ever seen.

As promised, Charlie had adjusted the containment area to match conditions outside the ship as closely as they were able. The creature should be relatively comfortable.

"Ok. Now what?"

It was almost like Jusef was reading Ray's mind. Ray shrugged. "No idea. Charlie?"

"We could try adjusting conditions, applying some stimulation. See how it responds."

Ray frowned as he considered Charlie's words. "What did you have in mind? I don't want to hurt it."

"Raise the ambient light level a bit?"

"I guess that can't do any harm. Go ahead."

Charlie nodded and turned to the containment area's control workstation.

Through the one-way viewing window, Ray could see the light levels increase perceptibly. They waited for several minutes, but nothing happened.

He nodded in response to a questioning look from Charlie, then waited as the other man raised the light level again.

Still nothing. Charlie raised the light level a third time.

The creature seemed to shrink in on itself and darken. That could not be good.

"Turn it down," Ray commanded, and within seconds Charlie had the lights back down to their original setting.

The creature slowly returned to its original size and, from what Ray could tell in the lower lighting, its original color. He breathed a sigh of relief that was echoed by the others with him.

"That was interesting," Jusef remarked.

The intercom beeped and Eva's face appeared on the display. She looked a bit worried.

"Ray, I just detected a burst of radio waves."

He could feel his eyebrows raising on his forehead. "Radio? From where?"

"Hard to say. The directional is not giving me a good reading. It's almost as if..." She frowned. "I'd say it came from us, but we haven't been transmitting." Something offscreen caught her attention and her frown deepened. "Another burst of radio. The directional got a read this time. It's..." Her eyes widened. "It's coming from the asteroid."

"What?"

Behind him, Margaret interjected, "Maybe we're not the first ones here."

Ray shook his head. "Not a chance. Did you hear of any other projects like ours?"

Silence was her answer. Ray looked around to see her biting her lip nervously. Finally, she shook her head. "What's causing it then?"

No one said anything for a long time Ray had a suspicion, but it was so unlikely...

He caught himself in mid-thought and gave himself a mental shake. Very little in nature was actually impossible. What if...

He looked back at the creature in the containment area and felt another surge of excitement.

"Eva, stand by," he said. "Charlie, raise the light level again, please. Slowly."

Charlie nodded, an eager light in his eyes. He suspected the same thing Ray did, apparently.

"What are you doing?" Margaret asked.

She moved forward from her observer's station to stand next to Ray, between him and Jusef. He glanced to the side, annoyance welling up for a moment. It was crowded enough without having someone pushing people around.

But then he saw her expression. Nervousness had given way to actual fear.

She *had* been out of the game for a while. He reminded himself that looking a new life form in the eye in the depths of space is far different from making policy decisions in an office in Washington, DC.

"Just watch," Ray said with a smile he hoped was reassuring. "This should be interesting."

The light level in the containment area gradually increased in response to Charlie's command. As before, nothing happened for a time.

Then, suddenly, the creature again shrank and darkened.

Charlie looked at Ray. "Turn it down?"

"Just a moment." Ray glanced at the intercom display. "Eva?"

Her reply was instant. "More radio transmissions, no good direction. What are you doing down there?"

"Confirming a hypothesis. Keep monitoring." With that, he turned back to Charlie and gestured for him to lower the lights again.

Very quickly, the ambient light in the containment area was back to its original setting. The creature reacted as it had before, returning to its original configuration.

"Any change, Eva?"

She nodded. "Radio transmissions have stopped."

"I'd say that confirms it," Jusef said with a grin. "They communicate with each other using radio waves."

"Astounding," Margaret breathed. Her nervousness was obviously fading. She leaned toward the viewing window to get a better look. "I've never heard of such a thing."

"It's not that unbelievable," Charlie replied. "Eels on earth can generate an electric current. It's not far from that to generating a radio signal."

"Yes, but to encode it, to make it coherent..."

Jusef snorted. "Let's not get ahead of ourselves. It's not like they're transmitting television or something."

Before Ray could interject, Eva gasped in surprise and shock over the intercom. He blinked; she was normally a very cool customer.

"Eva, what's up?"

"More transmissions from the asteroid," she replied. "The amplitude is more intense and the duration longer. I'm not sure what..." She looked at a display offscreen then cursed and went pale. When her gaze returned to the intercom, there was noticeable tension in her face and shoulders. "We've got a problem, Ray."

Eva tapped a command and her face was replaced with a view of the asteroid. It still tumbled slowly through space, carrying its unusual cargo. But Ray immediately saw what had caused Eva's chagrin.

Two green-brown blobs, larger than the others by several meters from the look of them, had detached themselves from the asteroid and were moving toward the ship.

"Aw hell," Charlie said. "It's Mom and Dad."

~

Back in the control room, Ray peered at the contact evaluation plot on the main display screen.

The two creatures were depicted as red Xs with velocity vectors displaying their speeds and projected closest points of approach to the ship. By most standards, they were not moving very quickly, just 5 meters per second. But they were on an intercept course with the ship and would arrive in less than three minutes.

"Now this is interesting," Ray said, looking from the plot to the camera display.

Detached from the asteroid, the creatures' undersides were visible. They had multitudes of flexible limbs that were capped by what appeared to be suction cups, but no mouth or eyes. Ears were out of the question, of course; they would be useless in the void. But where were the rest of the creatures' organs and tools?

They would be a fascinating study in a proper laboratory.

"I guess that's one way to describe it," Eva said. "What are we going to do? I doubt they're coming over for a friendly chat."

Charlie nodded concurrence. "If this is a display of parental protectiveness..."

"Or just a herd mentality," Jusef interjected.

Charlie sighed and nodded, conceding the point. "Either way, they're likely to be violent."

A loud snort was Margaret's initial reply. "They're floating blobs with suckers. How violent can they be?"

Ray tapped the command console and zoomed in on the asteroid, specifically on the grooves each of the creatures left in the rock. "Look at that, Margaret. I'm not sure we want to see what they can do to our ship's hull."

They sat in silence for a few seconds, considering. Glancing around, Ray saw frowns on every face.

There were no good decisions. They could just maneuver away; they could easily outrun the creatures at their current pace. But then they would lose the opportunity to study them in greater detail. They could release the creature down in containment and hope that, with its return, the others would calm down and go back to what they were doing. Or they could try to repel the approaching creatures.

Although exactly how they would accomplish that was another good question. Science vessels do not carry weapons, by and large, and this ship was no exception.

"I don't want to lose the opportunity to study them," Jusef said and received murmurs of concurrence from everyone in the room.

"Alright then. Jusef, try hitting them with the lights again, full spectrum this time." Jusef nodded but paused as Ray continued. "Charlie, go down to containment and get ready to bring the creature back outside." He noticed all eyes on him, none of them pleased, and he added. "Just in case."

Margaret scowled darkly but remained silent as Charlie got up and hurried out of the room.

It took a few keystrokes to reconfigure the strobes. By the time Jusef was ready, the creatures were two-thirds of the way to the ship. The tension in the control room was palpable by the time Jusef nodded in readiness.

"Ok, hit them."

At Ray's command, Jusef activated the strobes. There was an immediate reaction from the on-coming creatures.

They darkened, and the receiver indications at Eva's console lit up like a christmas tree as they transmitted their radio signal.

But they kept on coming. In fact, they increased speed.

Ray swallowed, a chill going up his spine as he looked at the plot and saw their speed had doubled. No wait, tripled. He keyed the intercom. "Charlie, are you ready?"

Charlie shook his head and Ray could see he was halfway into donning a spacesuit. "It's gonna be a couple minutes."

"We don't have a couple minutes. Hurry up."

Ray turned to Eva, who looked at the plot as though poleaxed. "Eva, move us away." She did not move, so he shouted more loudly, "Eva!"

Eva shook herself and acknowledged, then tapped in the sequence of commands that activated the ship's thrusters.

Ray felt a few seconds' acceleration, then in the main camera display, the asteroid began growing smaller. On the plot, the creatures' rate of closure reduced quickly and then went to zero.

"That will give us some time to think," Ray said, trying to sound more calm than he felt. "Jusef, turn the lights off."

"Already done." Jusef looked as though he really was calm. He tapped his index finger on his lips in thought as he watched the creatures on the display. "Very interesting. It's almost as though light hurts them, but also gives them energy."

"Yeah." Jusef was right. It was interesting. But it

was not the top priority at the moment. "I'm going to tell Charlie to release it from containment. Any objections?"

Eva shook her head quickly. Amazingly enough, Margaret was right behind her. Jusef looked for a moment as though he was going to raise an objection, but instead shook his head, frowning.

"Alright." Ray keyed the intercom again. "Charlie, as soon as you're ready, release it."

~

ON THE CAMERA DISPLAY, the small creature drifted away from the ship on its small asteroid fragment.

For a minute or so nothing happened. Then, all of a sudden, it detached from the hunk of rock. Several of the suction cups on the ends of its limbs made a burping motion and it began moving toward the two larger creatures.

They, in turn, altered their course toward it.

Ray let out a breath that he hadn't realized he'd been holding. "Looks like they're going for it," he murmured.

The creatures met and the smaller one made a tight circle around the other two, trailing its limbs over their backs in a strangely intimate display. After that, first one then the other larger creatures made a similar circle around the small one. The trio went on like that for several minutes, trading off circling caresses in sequence.

Then they stopped, clustered together in a tight formation.

"I guess that takes care of that... Aw hell."

Charlie could have been speaking for all of them. On the display, the small creature and one of the large pair split off and sped away back toward the asteroid, now just a small point of light in the distance. They moved far faster than before.

But the other large creature remained still for a long moment, then rotated in space and shot toward the ship, again at a much faster clip than it had used earlier.

"Crap," Eva shouted, and she punched the thruster controls.

They were pressed into their seats as the ship accelerated away, but the creature was was already going too fast. Inexorably, it grew larger in the display screen.

"Impact in thirty seconds," Eva reported, her voice strained but even.

"Any ideas?" Ray asked, and received silence in response.

Eva tapped another command and the ship lurched to the side, nearly throwing them out of their seats.

On the display, the creature zipped past, but quickly adjusted to their new vector as it continued to close the distance between them.

It was no use. They were going to collide.

"Brace for impact!," Eva shouted.

The creature filled the entire camera display, then the ship rang like a gong. They *were* thrown out of their chairs this time as the ship turned completely over. It took a long several seconds for the inertial systems to compensate and restore the gravity vector to normal, and they bounced around erratically the whole time.

When they finally came to rest, Ray came down hard on his left shoulder. Pain flared up from the joint and his arm went numb; a bad sign. Gritting his teeth to fight against the pain, he forced himself to his feet.

"Everyone ok?"

Assorted grunts and groans were the only answer. But one by one, the other three got to their feet. They looked alright. That was something, at least.

"Eva, status report please?"

Just then a loud hissing and popping sound echoed through the ship, followed by a deep groaning.

"What's that?" Margaret asked, her face ashen and her voice strained.

"My guess is the creature is trying to eat the ship, the same way it eats that asteroid," Jusef replied.

"Is there anything we can do?"

Great question. Ray looked over at Eva, who shook her head. "Short of doing an EVA and manually prying it off the hull, no."

"How long would that take?"

She snorted. "How do you intend to do it is the better question."

There was a long silence after that. Ray did a mental tally of their onboard equipment and was forced to concede her point. They did not have anything that could even begin to dislodge something as large as that creature.

"So we're screwed," Charlie summed up, apparently having done the same calculation in his head.

"Looks that way," Ray said. "Ok. Charlie, get all the data we've collected collated and transmit it to the Kranz Station. Eva, get the lifeboat powered up. The rest of you gather up your gear and all the food and water you can carry. There's no telling how long a rescue will take."

He rose and moved toward the door, but Margaret stepped in his way.

"This is insane. You can't know that it will be able to get through the hull."

"It's just a matter of time, if it keeps working at it."

"And what's to stop it from coming after us in the lifeboat?"

Ray sighed, feeling the others' eyes on him as he replied. "Nothing. Our best hope is that it's so focused on taking the ship out that it won't notice us when we launch."

"And if it isn't?"

He shrugged and her face dropped. He thought he saw the beginning of tears in her eyes for a moment. Then, with a swift inhalation, she wiped her eyes and nodded. "We'd better get to it, then."

Right then, in spite of himself, Ray found he admired her.

~

THROUGH THE LIFEBOAT'S viewing window, Ray watched as their ship died.

First one, then a second stream of gasses began venting from the vessel as the creature chewed through the hull and into the innards of the ship. The ship began rotating erratically under the force of the venting gasses and then, suddenly, blew apart in a quickly extinguished flash of flame.

The creature must have contacted the fuel lines.

Ray almost hoped the creature had been killed in the blast, but his intellect rebelled against such gross barbarity. It wasn't the creature's fault that they had come barging in to its home and carried off its child.

Jusef had earlier been quick to point out that there was no evidence the creatures were displaying family instincts, but Ray found he preferred to think they did.

It made them less alien and inscrutable, more human almost.

In the expanding ring of wreckage, Ray saw the creature right itself and rotate around in space for a moment. His breath caught in his throat.

This was it. Would it come after them again?

The seconds ticked by, each one seeming to take hours. Then, slowly, the creature began moving. Back toward the asteroid.

Ray breathed a sigh of relief and heard the same from his shipmates.

Smiling for the first time in what felt like years, he turned away from the viewing window. On the other side of the lifeboat, Eva had a set of earphones pressed to her ear. She nodded excitedly and said, "Roger, out."

Her smile as she turned to face the rest of them was like sunlight on a cloudy day. "They say the rescue will be here by this time tomorrow," she reported.

Combined with his relief over the creature's departure, the news made Ray feel like dancing a jig. Alas, there was not enough room for that. So he did the next best thing he could think of. Sitting down in one of the chairs that surrounded the table in the middle of the room, he looked his companions in the eyes one at a time and grinned.

"Anyone up for a game of cards?"

MESSAGE FROM THE AUTHOR

Thank you for reading my book. I hope you enjoyed reading it as much as I enjoyed writing it.

Every review helps an author out, so whether you loved this book, hated it, or something in between, please take a minute to tell other readers what you thought. All of the online retailers make it very easy to do, and I would really appreciate it.

Feel free to come say hi at my website or on Facebook. I always enjoy hearing from readers, especially since you all are, collectively, my boss.

I also have a weekly podcast, Story Time With Michael Kingswood, where I read stories and talk through some of the latest goings on in my world. I'd love to see you there.

Thanks again. My best to you and yours.

Warm Regards,
Michael Kingswood

MAILING LIST

If you enjoyed this book and would like word on new releases and special deals from Michael Kingswood, sign up for his newsletter on his website. Guaranteed to be spam-free, you can opt out at any time. And you can rest assured he will not share your information with anyone, for any reason.

https://michaelkingswood.com/newsletter-signup/

SUPPORTING PATRONAGE

Michael would like to invite you to become a supporting member of his website. Similar in concept to Patreon, a few dollars a month will give you access to exclusive content, and help him to focus more of his time to writing fun and exciting stories for your enjoyment.

Sign up at his website:

https://www.michaelkingswood.com/membership/supporting-patronage/

ABOUT THE AUTHOR

Michael Kingswood is 20-year veteran of the US Navy submarine force and a lifelong fan of science fiction and fantasy literature. His work has appeared in numerous collections and anthologies, to include the Fiction River Anthology series from WMG publishing. He holds a bachelors degree in Mechanical Engineering as well as a Master of Engineering Management and a Master of Business Administration. He has four children and currently resides in San Diego.

Find Michael Kingswood online at:

www.michaelkingswood.com

www.facebook.com/michael.kingswood

steemit.com/@michaelkingswood

MORE BOOKS BY MICHAEL KINGSWOOD

Glimmer Vale Chronicles

Glimmer Vale

Out-Dweller

Tollard's Peak

Robbed Blind

Wedding Gifts: A Glimmer Vale Chronicles Story

The Falconer's Stairs

Glimmer Vale Omnibus Edition #1

The Pericles Conspiracy

Passing In The Night

The Pericles Conspiracy

Dawn Of Enlightenment

Masters Of The Sun

Novellas

What Lurks Between

The Necromancer's Lair

The Champion

Veritas Morte

Story Collections

Tales Of Adventure #1

Tales Of Adventure #2

Short Story 10-Pack

A Jar Of Mixed Treats

Short Fiction

Michael has also published a number of shorter works,
links to which can be found on his website.

www.ingramcontent.com/pod-product-compliance
Lightning Source LLC
Chambersburg PA
CBHW032054180726
48284CB00004B/1331